The Busi
of
Retribution

Alex Ferguson

PublishAmerica
Baltimore

PublishAmerica has allowed this work to remain exactly as the author intended, verbatim, without editorial input.

ISBN: 1-60610-142-0
PUBLISHED BY PUBLISHAMERICA, LLLP
www.publishamerica.com
Baltimore

Printed in the United States of America

Prologue

A man walks through an airport terminal and approaches the back of the line at a rental car agency. As the line grows smaller the man in a dark business suit and green paisley tie waits patiently, neither drawing attention to himself nor refraining from making eye contact with the assorted people in line. The woman behind the counter, young with bright eyes smiles and asks, "How can I help you today, sir?" As the man hands her the identification in his wallet and tells her that he is here to pick up a car he has reserved. She begins typing into her computer, no doubt pulling up his reservation.

The young woman looks up bright eyed and takes a deep breath before she begins, "Mr. Marshall I have your reservation printing and I can show you a choice between a few models of the car you have reserved. Will you still need the car for three days?" As the man attempts to sound casual and rushed at the same time he replies with a grin, "Sure that will be more than enough time, just have a meeting at the corporate office and then back home." Smiling a patented smile the young woman rips the printed off paper from the printer and says with a practiced cadence to her voice, already starting for the door to the sea of parked cars, "Did you know that we are the preferred rental agency to hundreds of corporations across the country? We can sign you up for any number of programs that can save you time and money the next time you use our service in any town your travels may take you..."

"No that's quite all right, I don't plan on traveling enough to make it worth while, but I will let the folks at the corporate office know," said the man, Mr. Marshall for this purpose anyway. Without missing a beat the young woman continued as they wound their way from one endless ocean of newer model cars to another in an attempt to find the one car that this Mr. Marshall will be driving. Coming to a stop next to a silver sedan, the young woman begins her pitch for the optional insurance that she, of course, recommends to all her customers. Mr. Marshall not wanting to draw attention to him by taking time to explain that he will not need it accepts and signs the required documents. He gets in his rental, and with the young woman smiling and waving to him, he drives off without a care in the world.

A short time later an altogether different looking man pulls into the parking lot of a middle class hotel, and before stepping out of the car he checks his new look. With a wig of shoulder length blond hair and sunglasses, black t-shirt and jeans no one would ever suspect that this was the former Mr. Marshall, business man on a trip to the corporate office in his dark pin stripe suit. The man allowed himself a moment of pride as he saw himself in the reflection of the approaching glass door to the hotel lobby and marveled at how much someone can change from a simple alteration of their dress. As he approached the hotel front desk he went through the routine of checking in, this time as Mr. Carson.

"How long do you plan on staying Mr. Carson?" the attendant at the front desk asked.

"Only a few days, I am going to visit my sister who just moved here for a new job and see about helping her move into her new home" this Mr. Carson replied. "Also, I am thinking that I would like to sleep in after a hard day of moving furniture, do you have any rooms towards the back, preferably away from the pool?"

Looking at the console in front of him the clerk made a few adjustments to it and handing the man a key in the shape of a credit card while saying, "I have one that will fit your needs nicely. It's around the back, and bottom floor number 116."

After thanking the clerk at the front desk, and retrieving Mr. Carson's identification, the man went back outside and pulled the car to the parking spot in front of room 116. As he reached back to grab his luggage he looked around out of habit to see if anyone was paying particular attention to him before getting out of the car and opening the lock to his room and sliding through the doorway.

After a cursory inspection of the room, the man put his luggage on the bed and began changing yet again. He took off the wig replacing it with an Atlanta Braves baseball cap, and then he put on a light jacket and exchanged the sunglasses for nonprescription black rimmed ones. Checking through the window, he exited through the doorway as silent as he had entered. Once inside the car, the man checked his appearance in the rear view mirror and made his way out onto the empty street. The man looked in the glove compartment and found a map. After quickly identifying his location and looking at the map from the point of view of directions to an address which he had already memorized he began to navigate his way to his destination.

As the man made his way through a neighborhood that had seen better days he took notice of his surroundings. There were many middle class homes that had fallen into disrepair and neglect. Houses and lawns that had been unpainted and overgrown as though testifying to the world that their residents had either stopped caring or that the world has given up on them. Noticing one house in particular from the address that had been supplied to him, the man drove past and turned the corner to a nearby street and parked where he could keep surveillance on the home without being suspicious. As the man waited he quickly took off his jacket and cap stuffing them into his duffle bag along with the fake glasses. He then pulled out a brown paper bag that carried the tools of his trade. Like a doctor with his medicine bag, this man was the ultimate professional. He was methodical and precise, and never made a mistake. He was a man on a mission, and that certainty gave him all the comfort he would need for the task ahead. Checking the rear view mirror the man sees his target fumbling on the porch with an armload of bottles.

The former Dr. James Adams fumbled with as he attempted to manipulate the key into the lock of the front door. A task made all the more difficult by the armfuls of assorted alcohol he had wedged in his arms, carrying them as though they were nursing babes. The fact that he was completely trashed probably had nothing to do with it. Finally, he managed to open the door and stepped into the dismal one bedroom house. He stood in the doorway, teetering forward and backward and surveyed all that was left to him with bloodshot eyes. "Damn, it sucks to be home" he said slurring his words. As he shuffled across the sparse living room he kicked over empty bottles on his way to the comfort of his easy chair and his little flowers.

"Did you miss me my little flowers? Were you eagerly awaiting my return? Did you say to one another how you would be miserable until I came back to you?" he asked no one in particular. Dropping the bottles next to the easy chair the former doctor went the small coat closet in the hallway and pulled out a tape at random, then closed the door. Then, he shuffled over to the VCR and put the tape in, having to turn it around as he had at first attempted to put it in backwards in his inebriated condition. The once proud scientist then plopped down drunkenly unto the overstuffed chair, dust flying up into the sunlight making a cloud of filth in the air to match the rest of the house. He grabbed at the remote and fumbled with the buttons until the pitiful television set sprang to life. Managing to also turn on the VCR he settled in to watch one of his favorites. As he got more comfortable he looked to his right and saw the little red light blinking on his answering machine alerting him to more good news. With a wavering finger he pushed the play button and listened to the echoing voice of the woman who had become his only caller of late.

"Dr. Adams this is Danielle Bailey calling you for the fifth time this week. We still haven't received your payment, and as you know you are already two months behind on your –". She cut off as he angrily hit the delete button. *Damn her,* he thought. *Doesn't she know I am not a fucking doctor anymore?* He sighed as his memories came flooding back into reality. The life he had, one of importance. He was the best damn child therapist in the whole city, capable of doing miracles.

"I was the best!" he yelled at the answering machine. "There was no one who could make the little flowers smile and laugh like I could. No one could help them to experience the kinds of joy like I did! Damn you!" And yanking the answering machine from the end table, he threw it across the tiny living room smashing it against the far wall.

Taking ragged breathes and trying to calm himself from his burst of fury he realized that nature was calling. Taking a quick look at the trembling little girl on the television set, a young girl of about ten named Mindy, he remembered that this was one of the longer sessions he had with her and that he would have plenty of time to go to the bathroom and come back. As always, the little flowers were waiting for him.

Ponderously he struggled to get out of the chair as he made his way to the dingy bathroom. As he walked in he looked in the mirror and what he saw still shocked him even after all this time. Where once had looked back at him a robust man in his early thirties, now an old man who appeared more like sixty two rather than forty two. With grayish skin and withered hands, he dry washed his face and looked back into the mirror; that's when he noticed the man standing behind him.

He spun around and had to grab a hold of the sink that half supported him least he fall to the floor in his drunken state. He could feel panic welling up in his chest and bile in his throat. *Oh god, did he see anything on that tape?* he thought. His voice cracked when he shouted slurring his words, "Who the fuck are you? What in the fucking hell are you doing in my house" to the man who was now in front of him.

The man was dressed in dark blue jeans and a black tee shirt that showcased his toned physique. He had short black hair that was combed back, and though not quite as tall as the doctor, he still was not short. His hands where behind his back, and he was leaning nonchalantly with his shoulder against the door jam. The man gazed at the doctor with the appraising look of a cat that was deciding if the mouse it had just caught would be enough, or if it would have to continue hunting.

The man was not answering and in the silence of the house they could hear the tape continuing it's playing, and the two men could hear Mindy's pleas. "I don't want to Dr. Adams. Please don't make me do it again, it hurts!" The former doctor looked into the strange mans eyes, and saw the dark green of his irises begin to harden and boil. Taking his shoulder off the door jam he swung his arm from behind him and leveled the small pistol, equipped with a silencer at Doctor Adams knee.

"Call me Retribution, Dr. Adams." And with those words he squeezed the trigger and Doctor Adams heard the small metallic clink of the hammer hitting the firing pin right before he heard the meaty rip as his patella shattered and the bullet tore through the back of his leg, coating the floor of the bathroom with the ruins of the doctors knee.

Crying out in pain the doctor fell to the bathroom floor and grabbed at the mess that used to be his knee. He struggled to control his breathing but the searing pain was unimaginable. Attempting to cry out for help he opened his mouth to draw a deep breath and scream for someone, anyone to come and help him but before his shout could escape the man struck him with the butt of the pistol to the side of his throat, silencing the doctor. With the desperation of a wounded animal Doctor Adams struggled to get back on his feet. He put his hands on the toilet seat and tried to pull himself up oblivious of the dried piss on the rim. Upon hearing the tell tale metallic clink, and the explosion of pain in the doctors shoulder put an end to that idea. Writhing in pain on his bathroom floor, the doctor fell onto his back still choking from the strike to the throat the man had dealt him. He could feel the blood pulsing out of his joints where the man had incapacitated him.

The doctor knew enough to know that he was done. He would never leave here. He would die in this shit hole of a house in a pool of his own blood and now, with that realization, piss. Weakly, as his life was draining out of him, coughing he asked the man, "Who sent you to do this to me?"

The man was silent as Death, and in that silence the two men could hear Mindy on the tape crying, "Please stop, please stop."

The doctor shook his head in disbelief, tears beginning to run down his wrinkled face. "But, she loved me. She was my little flower. I brought her into womanhood to escape the torment of being a child!" Doctor Adams yelled defiantly.

The man looked down at Doctor Adams with Mindy's cries ringing in the background and said with steel in his voice, "She said that she wants you to suffer". And with that he shot the former Doctor Adams in the groin.

Before he could scream he found a towel stuffed in his mouth, and Doctor Adams was being pulled out of the bathroom by his mangled shoulder into the living room. His moans were muffled through the cloth but the tears of pain and self pity ran freely down his withered face just as his blood ran freely from his many wounds.

As he looked on in horror as the man went through his small closet in the hallway and pulled out a box. The box he held contained all the memories of his little flowers, and how the man, this Retribution knew to look for them there Doctor Adams would never find out. The man came back into the living room and ejected the tape and put it in the box as well, cutting off Mindy's cries. In the eerie silence, broken by the doctors muffled sobs the man pulled out a bottle, like the kind runners use to drink water from during a marathon and doused the box with what smelled like gasoline. After dropping the box and all its contents on the floor next to Doctor Adams the man struck a match and let it fall onto the box, and it immediately burst into flames and Doctor Adams could only watch his precious memories go up in smoke at his feet.

Then, with a hard look in his eyes, the look of true retribution, the man then began to pour the remaining gasoline on the doctor. With a renewed desperation the doctor tried to kick with his good leg but the man kicked him once in the injured knee causing a renewed agony and groans in the doctor until he submitted finally, nearly passing out from the pain and blood loss. The man, ever the professional took care to disarm any and all fire alarms in the house. Needlessly, there were few. Looking down as he approached his target, the man struck another match and watching it catch fire he looked upon the former Doctor Adams. The doctor could only catch a glimpse of the man's angular face through the smoke and flame as he let the match drop and as the now very former doctor was engulfed in flames a moment before he died.

Being careful to maintain his professionalism, the man took care when dismantling his tools. He pulled the disposable silencer that he had made the day prior apart from the gun he had used, and broke it in half. Then, the man, this personification of retribution pulled an ordinary brown paper bag out of his back pocket and placed the pistol and broken silencer in it to conceal them from anyone looking around as he made his way out the door and across the yard to the street where his rented car was parked. Starting the car, he slowly drove away without a care in the world.

Chapter 1
The Long Ride

Agent Curt Harvey walked through the sterile hallway to the elevator with a familiar sense of dread. Ever since being stationed at the main office, first floor it seemed to him that all reason for going to work was at an end. It wasn't that he didn't believe in the FBI anymore, it was just that this wasn't the FBI that he had lived in for so many years.

Where once he had been one of the elite; a top agent with the Behavioral Analysis Unit he was now reduced to checking backgrounds for potential agents and students looking to get visa's for studying abroad. In short, he has been humiliated and that's always the price for letting your ego get your team killed.

Just ten more years of this and I can retire, Harvey thought as he made what he had come to refer to as the walk of shame to his desk. Sitting down heavily in his faux leather chair he reclined and took inventory of the files that seemed to have somehow reproduced like rabbits all over his once meticulously arranged desktop. With a deep sigh Harvey let his eyes travel across to Agent Jennifer Hall, whose desk faced his, and wondered not for the first time how it must feel to still be a rookie agent and marvel at how lucky one can be with such a loathsome job such as theirs.

"You look like you could use this more than I could," Agent Hall said as she walked up and sat familiarly on the edge of Harvey's desk and pushed a cup of coffee to the edge of his desk so that it sat both inviting and precariously close to the edge.

"Does it have a new career at the bottom?" Harvey said taking a tentative swallow.

Rolling her eyes Hall blew a stray strand of her blond hair from the tip of her nose before replying, "Is this really so bad? I have never known someone who was such a pain in the ass as you are. In the four months that we have been partnered here you have done nothing but bitch and moan and complain. It simply can not be that bad here. Remember what Cooper said?"

"I remember, and I know that I should be grateful for his letting me come here but this isn't where I want to be for forever," Harvey replied.

Looking sad but determined Hall leaned forward, trying to catch Harvey's bloodshot eyes with hers to emphasize her point, "Don't worry, after all you are a brilliant agent, everyone fails at least once."

"But," Harvey replied, "Not everyone who fails as miserably as I did ever had to tell his best friends wife, and the rest of his teams families that he was the one who got them all killed."

"No, killed in the line of duty. Christ Harvey, you weren't the one who killed them" Hall said in a voice like she was trying to convince a child that they were not at fault for some wrongdoing.

I hope that he isn't broken, please God let him bounce back from this and be great and larger than life again, Hall thought before going on, "Look, you know probably better than anyone what dangers there are out in the field not to mention that when you came to speak at the Academy when I was a trainee you even said yourself that you can never know if the choices you make are the right ones, you just have to make the best ones given the circumstances, right?"

At that Harvey tilted his head back and rolled his eyes before closing them and kneading his knuckles against his eyelids. He felt the grit from the prior night's sleeplessness and overdrinking suddenly catch up to him. Suddenly he felt very tired of it all, and he didn't know if he had the strength to be at work, not just today, but if ever. *That does it, I am taking a leave and to hell with my guilt and self loathing,* Harvey thought.

"Look, Hall I am going to take a few days. You can handle all this," Harvey said while making a vague gesture that encompassed the whole floor, "and if Cooper asks just tell him I have the flu or something." Standing up out of his chair Agent Harvey grabbed a file from the stack on his desk and started past his partner. Before he got two steps from his desk he heard the words that would forever change his life.

"Harvey! Hall! I need to see you both in my office. Now." Special Agent in Charge Walter Cooper bellowed as he leaned his huge frame out of the door to his office before he turned and returned to his desk with the full knowledge that his agents would be in front of him in less time than it took him to think about it. SAC Cooper knew his agents and he knew the effect that he had on them. As a titan of a man, with a deep voice he knew that people jumped and paid attention when he made his wishes known. Couple that with an eerie resemblance to an African version of the Incredible Hulk and he was not someone his agents kept waiting.

"Yes sir?" Harvey said as he closed the door after Agent Hall had come in.

Don't fuck this up Harvey, SAC Cooper thought before he started, "Have a seat, but don't get comfortable. I have an assignment for you two." With a gravely voice Cooper continued, "I just got word that there has been an incident, and the word from the top is that they want you, Harvey, to be the agent on the ground for this. I have been pulling for you, and this is your one and only chance to get back into the normal rotation and maybe get your career back. I want you to take Hall here and give her some on the job training." Cooper then got up and pulled a file from the cabinet behind his desk. Handing the file to Harvey he took notice of the haggard look of his agent. Turning to Agent Hall, SAC Cooper said in a low voice, "Hall, get your gear and requisition a vehicle from the motor pool, we'll meet you in the garage."

"Yes sir!" Agent Hall replied before scooting out of the office with an excited grin on her face. SAC Cooper grabbed Harvey by the back of the neck with one of his enormous hands with surprising gentleness from a man so big and strong.

"Look at you Harvey," SAC Cooper said. "I was lead to believe that you were better than to succumb to letting yourself waste away with whatever the hell it is that you do at night. I need your best out here. Now tell me the truth; can you deliver?"

As Harvey took a deep breath and exhaled it through his nose he looked at the man who had chosen to believe in him when no one else would. Who took him when he was a broken shell of a human, much less a shell of a man. Who could have been Deputy Director had he not spoken up for Harvey when it was a possibility that he would have been facing serious repercussions for his egotistical behavior. With a jerk of emotion that Harvey didn't know he had a thought charged through his mind, *How can I let this man down?*

"Do I really look that bad, sir?" Harvey asked. "No, don't answer that. I will give you everything that I have and then some. You can count on me sir. I won't let you down."

"That's what I wanted to know. Follow me; I will brief you on the way to the garage."

SAC Cooper led the way out of his office with Harvey right behind him. The men made their way across the room to the elevator. Without preamble SAC Cooper began "What we have here is a class A cluster fuck, and I hope that you are ready for it."

As they waited for the elevator, Harvey let out a short chuckle, "Just like mom used to make."

"Laugh all you want, this is no joke. You know a local wise guy named Carlo Vacellaro?"

With that name Harvey looked up from the file he had just opened, "Are you kidding? He just got out of prison about two months ago. Heads the mafia and has been just as influential inside as he was while he was acting as boss. I hear that he is looking to retire, has he really done something to go back?"

"No, its worse than that. You heard that his daughter is getting married?" At Harvey's nod SAC Cooper continued as they stepped into the waiting elevator and hit the button to go to the garage floor, "Well, last night at the reception after most of the festivities were winding down he claims that most of his family, and by family I mean his crew, stayed at his place for the night. This morning the whole family wakes up to find that the old man's grand daughter, age eleven, had been raped and beaten. She is now being treated at the hospital. What I need from you is to take control if the situation and find out who the sack of shit is who did this, although I have a feeling that you will find out when you get there who they think did it. Apprehend his child raping ass and make sure that no one and I mean no one from Vacellaro's crew takes

19

matters into their own hands. I don't need the additional paperwork."

With that, the elevator door opened and they stepped out into the garage. As they walked to a waiting Agent Hall, Harvey turned to look at his mentor and best friend. "Don't worry sir. I will take care of this, and her."

"I know Harvey," SAC Cooper replied. "I wouldn't have asked you otherwise. Now get on the road and take care of business."

As Harvey got into the drivers side of the car with his partner he thought about the best way to bring her up to speed. He pulled out into traffic and took a deep breath. Naturally Agent Hall had been through the intense and demanding FBI training at the Academy and although she was green she was smart. The issue in front of Harvey as he saw it was how to get the best out of her. Training wasn't his strongest suit, but he was serious when he told Cooper that he would look out for her and he meant it. *Even if it means taking her into the lions den?* Harvey shuddered with the thought of his former team mates.

Agent Hall looked over at her partner and saw him lost in thought as he navigated his way through the late morning traffic. She thought of the best way to get Harvey to open up to her and also not appear over eager. "So, want to fill me in on the adventure?" Agent Hall asked.

Agent Harvey glanced at his partner and said in his best instructor's voice, "Since we have a long ride ahead of us I want you to pay attention and save your questions until I am done. First lesson is to listen closely, you never know what you will learn if you just let someone talk. Let them talk long enough and they will spill more than they intend to. Understand?" At her nod, Harvey continued. "No doubt you know who Carlo Vacellaro the head of the Italian mafia is. He was released from prison a short time ago and his daughter got married last night and they held the reception at his estate. When the party was over the guests stayed there, and this morning his eleven year old granddaughter was found raped and beaten. She is currently being treated and is at the hospital. From what I gather the local PD has requested our assistance and no doubt they are already there. We are to meet with them at the scene and gather what information we can and make haste with our arrest before Vacellaro can get his hands on whoever they think did it, and also investigate what actually happened. Now, what are your thoughts?"

Agent Hall chewed her lower lip for a moment before she answered. While she processed what little she knew of the situation, she thought of her training. It was too early to make a guess as to who the perpetrator was, so first think of how they could go about discovering who it could be. With a satisfied grin she answered confidently, "The first thing that I would do is look at who was there last night when everyone went to bed and isn't there now. That should give us an idea of who bolted last night after he committed the crime. It was most likely someone that the girl knew so he could get close to her without arousing suspicion and also be someone who wouldn't be missed if he were absent long enough to carry out the act."

Smiling at Agent Hall, Harvey had to admit that he was impressed. "Clever girl! I am going to tell you lesson number two. One of the hardest things to do as an investigator is to know that you don't know everything, and to realize that the pursuit of that missing knowledge is what makes a case come together. I see that you are at the head of the class already."

With such praise Agent Hall couldn't help but beam with pride. She knew that she was bright and had a logical mind, but to hear someone who was one of the best at investigating violent crimes and the methods criminals use tell her that she was doing exactly what she should be doing was more than she had hoped for. As the enthusiasm built in her she couldn't help but say, "So, when we solve this case and they let you back into the BAU do you think that you could put in a good world for me?"

With an optimism that he hadn't felt in a long time, Harvey replied, "Well, lets take care of one thing then the other, and if you continue to do as well as you have been I think that I might be able to reserve a spot for you."

Still elated, Hall said, "I think that I will learn a lot from you, and I want you to know I am going to take this very seriously."

As Agent Harvey pulled through the gates into the Vacellaro estate he saw the circus of police and news crews that had already infiltrated the grounds. After looking around at the bustling driveway he gave up and put the car into park and turned off the ignition. "Looks like school is in session Agent Hall. Lets go." And with that the two agents exited the car and began to wade through the crowd towards the front of the imposing mansion.

Chapter 2
Deals Struck

Lorenzo Silva walked down the long hallway of his employer all at once out of place and yet completely at home. The hallway ran the length of the second story, from the office to the bedrooms, and past the stairs. With gaudy and mismatched artwork adorning the walls there was ample evidence that the man who owned this magnificent home was by no means the most tasteful individual; with a recurring theme of bloodshed and battle in every painting it is easy to see that this is the home of a brute.

A distinguished looking man, Lorenzo was neither tall nor short, and he was always dressed immaculately. Like most of his fellow suit clad peers, he realized that he was born to look good as a mobster, instead of looking like a wild boar in Armani he made the look take on an air of sophistication that most mistook for being aloof.

Passing several doors along the corridor, he came to the end of his dreaded walk. After taking a deep breath and opening the door Lorenzo stepped into a room with the oppressive air of a concentration camp. As all the faces in the room looked at who would intrude upon their meeting place they immediately resumed whatever task they were busy doing, as Lorenzo only answered to one man in this Family of outlaws. That man, who was alternating between pacing the floor with his gigantic frame and stopping in mid stride to look about the room with a fire spitting fury. When Lorenzo cleared his throat to announce his arrival to his boss, Small Paul Vacellaro, the pacing stopped permanently. At Lorenzo's nod, Small Paul let out a deep breath and took a seat behind the large desk that occupied the room only less so than its owner.

"I assume that you have good news for me Silva?" Small Paul said as he leaned back in the leather chair. Noticing the other men in the room were taking care not to listen to the conversation, Lorenzo took the seat opposite the large desk and leaned back with his long legs folded before reporting his morning's malfeasance to his boss.

"Indeed. News of every kind even," Lorenzo said in a soft voice that belied the violence that he has caused in his fifty odd years. "It seems," he began, "That I was successful on all fronts. I have made contact with my cousin and he was already in route after the initial report from this morning. He should be joining us shortly."

Small Paul took the first opportunity to interrupt, "Does that mean that he is going to help our efforts or make life difficult?"

What do you think you great big stupid piece of shit? Lorenzo thought to himself with a perfect poker face. But instead of voicing his opinions he simply put his boss at ease, "No he is on board with our plans, and will make the necessary arrangements with the local FBI when they arrive, which too should be shortly."

"The FBI is coming here?" asked one of the nameless soldiers that littered the room like so much useless trash.

Turning his head in the general direction of the interruption but still maintaining eye contact with Small

Paul, Lorenzo replied, "This was all part of the plan, which, you were left ignorant like so many other things in life."

After a general murmur of laughter, which broke off abruptly when Small Paul glared around the room Lorenzo continued, "Also with good news, I was able to make contact with someone to clean up this little problem for us. Before you ask he is a professional at what he does, and this kind of thing seems to be his specialty. He said that he was close by and will be here within the hour. I don't think that you will be disappointed."

"Excellent work Silva, as always you fail to disappoint."

"Then you won't like this," Lorenzo started, "It seems that from a contact I have in the FBI, they are sending some former member of one of their high and mighty unit. Used to profile serial killers or something." After telling Small Paul this news he watched his not too intelligent boss to see if there would be any effect, and was not surprised to see the expected result. Upon hearing this, Small Paul got visibly disturbed, and for good reason. *Now we will see what you have to say for yourself, you fucking idiot.* Lorenzo thought. As he saw this look of comprehension come upon Small Paul's face, he realized that there was more to what happened last night than even he had been made aware. And if what Lorenzo had suspect was in any way true, then he would have to be sure and tell his cousin that there would be an opportunity for them both.

After Small Paul had collected himself with a brief clearing of his throat he said more loudly than was necessary, "Then I suppose that either your beloved cousin or our cleaner will have more work to do. I will leave it in your capable hands to decide which."

With no time for a reply, Lorenzo's attention was taken back to the rear of the room as a knock at the door prefaced the housekeeper coming into the room before she said, "Excuse my interrupting sir, but there is a Detective Silva in the hallway who would like to speak to you."

Without waiting for the okay, Lorenzo got out of his chair, "Thank you please let him in." Right then a man who was obviously related to the Silva family came through the door. He calmly took in the surroundings, and if he realized the shark infested waters that he was treading he did not show the least bit of fear, and as with most men named Silva he had a soft and even voice when he said, "Thank you for seeing me Mr. Vacellaro, you and your family have our undivided resources."

At that Small Paul got up and stood to his most imposing height as he walked around to stand face to face with the slender detective. Small Paul started, "I appreciate your coming here, and I know that this investigation will be in good hands. I trust that you will see that we have mutual interest in this situation being resolved, and also that we will be," Small Paul paused before saying in his most menacing tone, "free of any need for federal interference."

With an almost imperceptible smile and a glance at his cousin Lorenzo, Detective Daniel Silva replied with his trademark cool, "There is no reason for the fed's to get involved, but with certain interest in your business dealings I am sure that they will send someone to consult. So long as that is all that they do, I can assure you that as the lead detective on this case I will be able to ensure that their interference is minimal." Now that the verbal fugue was out of the way, Lorenzo took his cousin by the shoulder and motioned him to the doorway he had only just come from with an unspoken dismissal. As the two men walked out of the office, they remained quiet until they were down the hallway near the top of the stairs leading to the main entryway of the house.

"What I don't get is why this all happened in the first place," Detective Silva said to his cousin. "With it being such a crowded place and the big bosses own niece and all, you would think that someone would have more sense."

Choosing his words carefully Lorenzo admitted, "You don't know the kind of animal some of these men are, and in particularly the one we suspect. As we discussed on the phone, I am sure that you know who Frank the Tank Cislo is?" At the detective's nod he continued, "We assume that he is the one, as he was the only one who left the party before anyone woke up this morning. Of course, we don't know exactly where he is, but you are the detective are you not?"

"Is he still the one playing at being a big time pimp? Yeah I got a few ideas. I remember a few years ago when he got run in for whipping one of his girls, he beat her so bad she was in the hospital for a few weeks. Stupid woman wouldn't press charges though."

"He serves for other tasks, and they aren't the kinds that require manners." Lorenzo replied. As his cousin shook his head and holding up his hands, letting Lorenzo know that he didn't want to hear anymore he started down the steps to the front door.

"You just be careful, I got a hunch that there is more here than either of us know—"

"But we suspect you and me." Lorenzo finished, as was their habit since growing up. Smiling, the two men went their separate ways before Detective Silva stopped at the foot of the staircase. He turned around and said with a genuine note in his voice, "I saw your boy last weekend when I was at the school on another matter. He is a good looking young man, and you and Kelly should be proud. Coming over for dinner this Christmas?"

"I wouldn't miss it for the world, and thank you. Just be careful out there." Lorenzo said.

Laughing slightly, Detective Silva said as he walked out the front door, "And you be careful in here!"

Looking at the door as it shut behind his cousin, Lorenzo was turning to go back to the office when he noticed the housekeeper making her way towards him up the stairs with a frightened look on her face. "I am not sure who to tell this to, but there was a man who came in through the kitchen saying that he is here to see Mr. Vacellaro."

"Take a second to collect yourself," Lorenzo said coolly before he saw a man come up the stairs. Immediately Lorenzo could see how the housekeeper could have been startled. The man was known to him only by reputation, but even that could not have prepared him for the cold professionalism that emanated from the stranger. As Lorenzo summoned all of his will, he walked towards the man who would for no reason other than monetary gain, kill anyone who could afford it. As he approached the man he noticed that he was taller than average, and though not bulky he was solidly muscular even under the business suit the man wore, no doubt to fit in with the crowd at the mansion that morning. "I take it that you are the man I contacted earlier?" Lorenzo asked.

With a solemn nod of the head the man, otherwise said nothing. As the two men stood for a moment looking into one another's eyes and sizing one another up the silence between them was broken by Small Paul coming out of the office and proceeding down the hallway. Lorenzo took stock of the man before him, noticing with surprise that the man did not look at all startled or unnerved at the sudden appearance of the most feared crime boss in the city. As Lorenzo turned to his boss, he made introductions between the two men, "Don Vacellaro, allow me to introduce the man I told you about, I am sorry I didn't get your name?"

"Never mind names, Silva. I am sure that there is no need for us to know one another or be on a first name basis. Just know I want the perverted fuck who did this to die and send me the bill." With that Small Paul brushed past the two men and the man noticed a huge ring on Vacellaro's finger, with diamonds in the shape of a "V" before Vacellaro and his entourage made their way past the two men and on down the hallway towards the stairs and down to the kitchen.

As Lorenzo found him self once again alone with the stranger he found his composure and remarked before saying, "The man you are looking for is named Frank Cislo. He is an associate of ours, and left the reception either early this morning or late last night. We don't know for sure where he is and with all the police presence here we can't send anyone out to look for him, so largely this task will be yours as well." Turning and walking back to the office Lorenzo grabbed a piece of blank paper from Small Paul's desk and after writing a phone number on it, he handed it to the man who had followed him so quietly that Lorenzo was momentarily flustered to find the man right behind him. "This is the number of the lead detective on this case. He will be able to update you on any information that will lead you to the whereabouts of Frank." As the man took the number without looking at it and put it in his coat pocket. As a complete shock to Lorenzo, the man asked a question with a voice that seemed to be all at once strong and dispassionate, "Why is it that this…Frank would beat and rape the head of the largest crime family in the metro area's niece right here in this house?"

Before replying, Lorenzo took a deep breath "You are not the first person to ask that question. I can't know why animals do what they do, but I am sure that we will never have to ask that particular question again. Do we have a deal?" As the man looked at Lorenzo's hand he took it and when they shook on their agreement, Lorenzo felt a chill run up his spine.

* * *

Detective Silva emerged from the mansion into what looked like uncontrolled chaos. There were news vans and reporters and various police personnel trying to maintain some sense of order all over the front of the estate and beyond. While standing on the porch, Detective Silva noticed a pair of people, one man, and one woman approaching him. They were obviously by their suits and firearms the federal presence he was going to have to deal with, but he wasn't expecting what he saw. The man walking towards him was apparently the seasoned one of the two as the woman must have just gotten out of training. She was a cute woman and had a bounce in her step that clearly indicated that she was on her first assignment. *This should be more fun than a root canal* Detective Silva thought sarcastically to himself. He met the two FBI agents partway down the long path that ran from the door to the driveway and introduced him self, "I am assuming that you two are from the Bureau? My name is Detective Daniel Silva and you are?"

Offering his hand in one hand and in the other flashing his badge, the man replied, "I am Special Agent Curt Harvey, and this is my partner Special agent Jennifer Hall. Are you the lead detective here?"

"Yeah," Detective Silva answered, "And I know that you have to be here but I would just as soon not have to argue over who has the authority here after all this is not something that the FBI usually handles."

Agent Harvey smiled and said, "We are only here to consult due to a specific invitation from your department. Just let us know how we can help."

"Sounds like a deal to me," replied Detective Silva as a uniformed police officer ran up to him and said, "Detective Silva, we have a lead."

Chapter 3
Apprehended

Detective Silva turned to the two FBI agents with an uncharacteristic smile on his face. "I swear it's never this easy," he said taking a slip of paper from the officer.

Detective Silva started towards his car with the two agents following closely behind. Turning to them while still making his way through a crowd of police officers trying to keep the assorted press at bay he said, "I don't know how you normally do it, but I like to kill two birds with one stone. What do you say you and I take a look into this lead," as he pointed towards Agent Harvey, "and you go to the hospital and see if there is anything from the girl," pointing then towards Agent Hall.

Harvey nodded as he said, "Sounds good to me. Do you know where we are headed?"

"Yeah, I had an idea that we would be looking for a particular fellow, so on my way here I made a few calls and put out an APB to see if this guy would turn up. Looks like we just got a nice break." As detective Silva went to open the door of his car he looked over the roof as Agent Harvey handed some keys to the female agent and was about to get into the passenger side. "What are you doing?" Silva asked.

"Sorry?" Agent Harvey said as he stopped before getting into the seat.

"Why don't you just follow me there in your car, that way we can split up if we need to." Silva answered.

"We only brought one car here, so I guess you're stuck with me," Agent Harvey said with only trace annoyance in his voice.

"No problem, I just thought that it might make it easier if we went in different cars, feel free to get in and hold on tight though, I don't want this jerk off to get away." Silva stated as he got in, buckled his seat belt and turned the ignition.

As they pulled out from the crowded driveway, the two men entered into an uncomfortable silence until Agent Harvey said, "So, they don't have you partnered with anyone?"

Looking sideways at his passenger Detective Silva replied, "No one as cute as your partner. No, mine is taking a leave to handle some personal business and has been for about a year and half now."

"I'm sorry to hear that, I can only imagine that it must be a difficult situation." Harvey said as he well knew that when a partner took a leave of absence like that, there must be some tragedy involved. *And wasn't I about to do something similar not two hours ago?* Harvey thought.

"Well, you know what they say: Shit Happens."

"Don't I know it," Agent Harvey replied before he began, "So, want to tell me the story? What kind of pile of shit am I about to step into?" *Make him your friend, use the same terminology and mannerisms and he will think that you are on the same page and maybe he will let something slip,* Agent Harvey thought, instantly getting back into profiler mode.

"It's pretty simple. I interviewed someone at the mansion, and he told me that the only person not accounted for was some lowlife thug slash wanna be pimp name Frank "The Tank" Cislo. I happen to know who this guy is and what he is capable of. I am afraid to say that I am not in the least surprised."

"Someone at the mansion?" agent Harvey asked? "How reliable is this information, or for that matter the person that you got it from?"

With a noticeable drop in temperature Detective Silva prepared to defend himself for what seemed like the millionth time and began in a voice barely above a whisper, "I know that you might not know this, but I haven't had a very easy time becoming a detective. You see," Silva looked right at Agent Harvey, "My cousin Lorenzo, who is like a brother to me, works directly for Carlo Vacellaro. I am very proud of my cousin, but not of some of his choices. Now that you know that, rest assured that I have been investigated by everyone from my former partner, to Internal Affairs, and even some of your buddies at the FBI." Looking back towards the road, and taking a deep breath Detective Silva let the weight of what he had just said sink in as they pulled out onto the main highway.

Holding his hands up in mock surrender, Agent Harvey replied, "Whoa, I had no idea. That sounds like a terrible situation to be in, and I don't envy you. If you have been through the meat grinder by all of them, I am certainly not anyone who is going to call you out." *Remain calm, validate him, see where he wants to take this,* Agent Harvey thought without realizing that he was getting back into the all too familiar thought processes he never imagined he would need again.

"Sure. Hey, no hard feelings okay? Its just one of the buttons that I have had pushed too many times in too many years."

Giving Detective Silva a smile to ease the tension, Agent Harvey said, "Well, I know that it would have been impossible to be an agent with that kind of family, so I can appreciate how hard you have had to work to get where you are in a big city like this."

Grunting in acknowledgement and looking to change the subject Detective Silva started, "So, the guy we are looking for is named Frank "The tank" Cislo and they don't call him that because he is a small pushover of a guy. He has a girlfriend who lives in an apartment here in town. Sometimes he pimps her out, and sometimes he just beats her. But if I was him, and looking to hide out or collect myself before getting out of dodge then that's where I would go first. If he isn't there, then undoubtedly she will know where he is."

"Does she have a name?" Agent Harvey asked with a note of caution in his voice considering the conversation they had just moments earlier.

With a sarcastic tone Detective Silva replied, "She isn't any relation to me, but she calls herself Honey."

Detective Silva pulled off the highway and took a few alley roads to a decidedly sleazy part of town. They passed several buildings that looked like they either should be or were condemned; there was little doubt in Agent Harvey's mind that if he was someone who was on the run from the mob and the law there was few better places that a person could disappear into.

The two men pulled over on a side street, and got out of the car. As Detective Silva gave the dispatcher his location and took his portable radio from the dock, Agent Harvey checked his weapon and tried to get his racing heart under control.

"So, what should I expect?" Agent Harvey asked.

Detective Silva looked over the roof of the car and replied, "Nothing too intense, after all we don't even know for sure that he is here. I can tell you that if Honey is here alone and knows where he is we might be in for a fight if he has been here and left."

"Okay, let's do this." Agent Harvey said and followed Detective Silva to a particularly dingy and pathetic looking building.

The two men walked into the building and took inventory of their surroundings. The lobby was empty except for the two of them and a number of rats walking around the floor. In the flickering light they could see that an elevator door was missing but had been replaced by yellow caution tape, presumably so no one would walk into the empty elevator shaft on the ground floor. Agent Harvey tried not to gag on the sour milk smell as he took the left half of the lobby to Detective Silva covering the right. The unlikely partners found their way to the stairway and proceeded to make their way up the floors, with Detective Silva saying the number thirty-four C and pointing up to the third floor. As they went up the stairs they heard a variety of music, yelling, fighting, and other noises of low class scum living their lives.

Coming to the third floor landing Detective Silva peeked through the door and led the way down the hallway to a door towards the opposite end marked 34C. Before the two men got to the door they could hear a man and woman yelling and sounds like someone was throwing object around the apartment. Posting up on either side of the door Detective Silva and Agent Harvey waited and listened to the broken conversation between what appeared to be Frank Cislo and Honey.

"...where I am going to go but it has to be somewhere far...," from the male voice.

This was followed by a female voice saying, "Are you fucking crazy coming here? They are never going to believe that I don't know where you went you asshole. They are going to fucking kill me!"

Then there was an unmistakable sound of stomping footsteps and a meaty smack as someone yelled "Bitch" and a body crashing into the wall right next to the door. Without hesitating the two men kicked in the door and brandishing their weapons pointed them directly at the man standing not a few feet from them.

Calling for the man to freeze, Agent Harvey assessed the man before him. He was a large man and though he was short he was powerfully built, like he could run right through a wall and not even slow down. He was breathing hard, and sneered at the two men in front of him as he looked over them with his beady eyes. Agent Harvey could tell that Frank was considering rushing them and maybe dying, but instead threw up his hands saying, "Fuck it. Take me or don't, I'm dead anyway."

Agent Harvey moved behind Frank and handcuffed him before reading him his rights and leading him out the door and into the hallway. At the same time Detective Silva was tending to the woman who was crumpled against the wall. Noting that she was coming around, Detective Silva nodded to Agent Harvey to take their captive downstairs.

Pulling the radio from his belt, Silva called in, "We have apprehended the suspect Frank Cislo, and have him in custody. Also, requesting medical attention for one female who has sustained blunt force trauma..." he cut off as he noticed his cell phone buzzing at his side. He didn't recognize the phone number but he knew who it would be. Looking at Honey and seeing that her eyes were still unfocused, Silva answered his phone.

"Detective Silva here," he said.

"You have something that I want," said a monotone male voice on the other end.

"What you want just walked out of this building with the FBI." Thinking that he should let the unknown person on the other end know that he was on board Detective Silva continued, "Don't worry, when I find out where he is being kept I will call you. How do I get in touch with..." Before he could finish his sentence, the man on the other end of the phone hung up.

Swearing under his breath Detective Silva continued giving information to the dispatch officer. When he was done he looked around the apartment while waiting for the paramedics to arrive. Noticing that the whole place looked like it had been turned upside down, Detective Silva proceeded to comb through the mess. Just as he was pouring through the remains of the living room and finding nothing he noticed by the door that Honey was coming back to full consciousness.

Kneeling down beside her, Detective Silva held her hand as he had many times while taking her statements in various hospital rooms and other less pleasant locations in the few years he had known her. When her eyes regained their focus and she realized who he was she let out a groan and started to tear up.

"It's okay Honey; he is not going to hurt you anymore." Silva said in his soft voice. Slowly putting his arms around her, and rocking her back and forth as Honey sobbed silently he tried to comfort her as much as possible. *This is the part that makes my life so unbearable,* Detective Silva thought.

After a few minutes Honey had regained her composure and started to get up. Helping her to her feet, Detective Silva made sure that she was steady before asking her, "Are you going to be okay? The paramedics are on the way and they will take care of any injuries that you have."

"Thanks Silva but I think that I will be okay," Honey replied before she pushed him away. "Where is Frank?" she asked.

Taking a deep breath to steel him for a possible confrontation Detective Silva said, "He is downstairs now, in custody. I am sure that before tomorrow he will be indicted for the assault and battery, and rape of a child. Fuck Honey! What the hell was he thinking?"

Honey looked at Detective Silva, and shook her head, "What are you talking about, rape of a child?" she said. "He has never done anything like that, and I would know. He wasn't the one who did that to Vacellaro's niece."

"I am afraid that you are mistaken Honey. He was the only one who was missing this morning when…"

"He was gone before this morning Silva. He left after the reception to take care of some business; I know because I called him and picked him up. Also I was with him the whole time. I came home about an hour before he did, and when he came back he was tearing through the place trying to find enough money to get out of town. He TOLD me what happened, and I begged him to leave and not get me involved. That's when you came in."

"Holy shit Honey," detective Silva replied. "You better make like Frank and get out of town or they are going to come after you, especially whoever it was that really did it." At that, Detective Silva took some money out of his pocket and put it in her hand.

"You still don't get it do you *Detective*. It was Vacellaro. Frank told me that when Vacellaro got out of prison he asked Frank to get him some girls, and by girls I mean little girls. Frank was in the process of doing just that last night before all hell broke loose. Now do you see how fucked I am," Honey cried.

"That does it," Detective Silva said, "We are getting you out of here now. Come with me," and pulling Honey out of the apartment they ran down the hallway and down the stairs outside to the car.

Before Detective Silva could explain the situation to Agent Harvey, several police cars and an ambulance had arrived on scene and he heard the FBI agent on his cell phone telling someone on the other end that they had apprehended Frank Cislo. What he didn't know at the time was that they had apparently apprehended the wrong man.

Chapter 4
Confessions

Y ou need to leave now," Detective Silva told Honey. "If you have anywhere in the world to go, get as far away as you can because I have a feeling that I am not going to be able to protect you, not from this."

As Honey got in the ambulance she nodded her understanding. Certainly she would be able to leave now that Frank was being taken to jail, and if she didn't leave, she would be dead in a matter of hours. What she knew was too sensitive and would damage some very violent people.

Detective Silva made his way to Agent Harvey, who was just finishing a call and put away his cell phone. The two men looked at one another with one looking satisfied, and the other looking mortified.

"Not bad for two guys who never met one another before an hour or so ago wouldn't you say Detective?" Agent Harvey said holding out his hand to shake. Taking Agent Harvey's hand, Detective Silva pulled his new partner close and whispered in his ear, "We have to talk. Now."

Detective Silva and Agent Harvey walked a short distance away from the hustle and bustle of news cameras, reporters and police. Once Detective Silva was sure that they were far enough away he leaned in close and said, "We have arrested the wrong man. While I was up there with Honey, she told me everything that had happened last night."

As Agent Harvey looked at the seasoned detective he had half expected to hear this. Surely, there was some sense of duty that Detective Silva felt towards the victims of violence in his city. As he listened to the cop tell him of the conversation upstairs in the apartment he saw so many pieces fall into place. *Even after everything I have been through, seen so much and lost almost my entire career the writing is plain on the wall. He is transferring and it's textbook,* Agent Harvey thought to himself.

"Silva, listen to what you are saying. Now, listen to what I am going to say. Honey has been abused by this man for years. She has never, not one single time pressed charges on him, right? Is it any surprise to you that she would try and defend him in this situation? He is going to go to prison for a long time and there is every chance that she will never see him again. She would say *anything* so that doesn't happen."

Agent Harvey shook his head and continued, "I have seen it too many times and I am an expert in human behavior. I could have told you that this was going to happen."

Detective Silva looked into his eyes and told him with his trademark cool, "And I am an expert in Honey's behavior and she has never lied to me. That man in the car, yes, he is an animal but he didn't do this."

Shaking his head once again the FBI agent replied "It isn't going to play out that way and my boss just got here and I think that he is going to want to hear what you have to say for himself."

"If it means that we get the right guy then let's do it" the detective said.

As the two men walked towards the black SUV that had just pulled up a huge man stepped out and walked to meet the two men. When they were only a few feet apart the SAC introduced himself to the detective, "I am Special Agent in Charge Walter Cooper and it is a pleasure to meet you."

Detective Silva shook the Special Agent in Charge's hand and said, "Sir we have a serious problem here. It seems that there is some contradictory evidence in this case."

As the detective filled in SAC Cooper on his conversation with Honey in the apartment a look of disgust filled the large man's face.

"You mean to tell me Detective," said SAC Cooper "that *if* this is in any way true, you just let that woman get away without so much as giving a statement?"

"It was in her best interest sir, she is not safe anywhere…"

"Fucking Christ Detective Silva! How am I supposed to corroborate her statement if she doesn't even give one nor is she here to give it? Harvey? Get this Frank fellow downtown and see what he has to say. We'll take it from there. Detective, this case is now in the hands of the FBI and I will suffer your presence only as much as I need to." Turning away SAC Cooper walked back to the SUV and said over his shoulder, "Call your partner Harvey, get her down here and fill me in on what you find. I swear to God I don't want to hear of any more fuck ups."

"Yes sir," Agent Harvey said to a retreating SUV. As he pulled out his cell phone to call Agent Hall, he noticed Detective Silva taking a call. He pushed the speed dial on his phone and as a matter of habit tried to listen in on the others conversation.

"Agent Hall? Harvey, what have you got for me?" As he listened to his protégé tell him that the little girls condition had gotten worse and that she may not make it, he overheard Detective Silva on his phone, "I don't know yet...I will...how do I? Shit," he said as he hung up.

"Yeah I got that," Agent Harvey said "just meet me back at the bureau and I will bring you up to speed. And Hall, I need someone here that I can trust."

As he hung up Agent Harvey walked up to the detective and said, "Ready to see what this guy has for us?" Watching for any clue as to what the conversation was about Agent Harvey couldn't see any cracks in the big city cops cool exterior.

"Let's see if we can get a confession," Detective Silva replied.

Back at the FBI building Agents Hall and Harvey were standing in the hallway by the interview room with Detective Silva recounting the events of the day. As Agent Hall learned about the apprehension of Frank Cislo and subsequently the conversation between Honey and the Detective she filled them in on the girl she checked on at the hospital.

"She isn't doing well, and considering the amount of damage that she has sustained it is surprising that she is even alive." Agent Hall said. "Not only is there the obvious rape trauma but she has had several fractures to her skull from a blunt object, I have pictures coming as soon as they come in I will get them for you. The attending doctor says that she may not regain conscience and even if she does there may be permanent brain damage."

"Then obviously," Agent Harvey said both to Detective Silva and Agent Hall "We will need to get a confession, or at the very least find out what the hell happened."

Taking a deep breath Detective Silva spoke up "I know that this is your turf, but it is still my investigation. I have talked to Frank many times and I know him well. It might be for the best if I am the one to do the interrogation."

Agent Harvey replied, "I can think of a few thousand reasons why that's a bad idea, but right now I don't need my boss asking me why he won't talk to us while you are sitting out here. So, just get him talking then I will take it from there and let's see if he has the same story as Honey."

"Let's do this then," Detective Silva said as he opened the door into interview room two.

The two men walked in to find a very agitated Frank Cislo. He was handcuffed with his massive arms behind his back and also with his ankles shackled together. As they walked into the room and shut the door, not saying a word, Frank Cislo took it upon himself to start the conversation, "You guys don't have a fucking clue how bad of a mistake you are making."

"Why is that?" Agent Harvey said as he took the chair opposite the furious prisoner.

Detective Silva leaned against the wall and said, "Seems like we got the right guy, after all you did disappear last night and everyone at the party seems to think that you are the guy."

Tapping his heel rapidly on the interview room floor, Frank let out a huge sigh and gritted his teeth before he replied. "You know me better than this *Detective Silva*. I am no saint, but I don't perv on kids. Not my style. Besides, I would expect that your cousin would say anything to protect that fucking slime boss of his."

Letting out a snort of disdain Detective Silva shook his head and remarked, "Seems like he is your boss too, but why don't you enlighten us as to what happened."

"Fuck off Silva, I don't have shit to say to you, or the G-Man here" Frank said nodding towards Agent Harvey who had sat back in his chair studying the man on the other side.

He is not avoiding eye contact nor is he stuttering his words. He is nervous and frightened of something more than the prospect of going to prison. Not what I would expect from a brutal sociopath, Agent Harvey thought. As he began making mental notes on his subject Agent Harvey decided now was the time to try and catch him off guard.

"Frank, look at yourself," Agent Harvey said. "You're a nervous wreck and from what I have heard this isn't the first time that you have laid a beat down on a woman."

Frank snarled as he replied, "I might have smacked some of my women around, but I like a little grass on the field when I play ball. Fuck. Right before you two showed up I had a few lines of the Devils Dandruff if you know what I mean. I wasn't even at the God damn party when this all went down. No, I was out trying to…umm…oh shit. Look, I was told that Vacellaro wanted to get some party favors for later and he is the one who likes them young."

With a raised eyebrow Agent Harvey pushed a little, "Who in the world would have asked you something like that?"

"Fucking Vacellaro himself! Why do you think that I left to do it immediately?" Frank replied.

With his cool voice dripping ice Detective Silva asked "Is there anyone who can corroborate your story Frank?"

With a grunt Frank said, "You know damn well there isn't. Not only that but I am sure that Honey is halfway to fucking China right about now no thanks to you."

"Funny," Detective Silva said "She didn't say anything to us about going to China. Are you sure that you got your fact straight Frank?"

"So now I am the comedian? Go fuck yourself Silva. You and I both know that you have been wanting to rub your wood on that for years now." Frank said.

Losing his cool Detective Silva rushed towards Frank and grabbed him by the collar and barked, "You pathetic piece of shit! You deserve being left alone by someone you beat on so bad that she had to be hospitalized. How many times do you think you're going to be fucked in prison Frank? I hope they let me be the one to fry your ass if that little girl dies, because I am going beg and plead and call in every favor just to be the one to flip the switch."

Just then there was a knock on the one way glass, the cue for the interview to stop. Agent Harvey got up and took Detective Silva by the shoulder before saying, "Let's go Detective. There will be plenty of time for this later."

Regaining his composure the cool exterior came over the detective and he released the prisoner and straightened his jacket before running his hand through his hair and taking a deep breath. Without a word he turned and walked out of the room with Agent Harvey behind him.

In the hallway stood Agent Hall who was looking at the floor and chewing her lower lip and SAC Cooper who looked less than impressed.

The huge FBI SAC shook his head and said with his deep gravely voice, "Just what the hell was that Detective?"

With a cool voice that never wavered Detective Silva replied, "In case you didn't notice he just corroborated Honey's story, down to the last detail. Sir."

Crossing his arms over his broad chest SAC Cooper looked right at the detective and said, "You know just what I mean. You have stretched my patience to the limit and as of right now your involvement in this case is through."

Detective Silva never looked away from the big mans eyes as he replied; "You're making a huge mistake. I am the only one who knows all these people and I am the only one who can make this case for you. I *know* what their next move will be and I *know* how to get this wrapped up without anyone else getting hurt."

SAC Cooper looked as though he had been slapped in the face before he said, "The only thing that I know is that your cousin is a ranking member of the very crime family we are currently investigating and that of all people you should be as far from this as possible. I want you out of this building with all haste *Detective*."

At this moment Agent Harvey interjected, "Sir, we still don't have enough to charge Frank Cislo with this and we can't just let him go."

Turning towards his agent SAC Cooper said, "Take him to a safe house and put him in protective custody until we can figure this out. I want this wrapped up before tomorrow and Harvey,"

"Sir?"

"Escort Detective Silva from the building."

Chapter 5
Not So Safe House

As the two men walked out of the building Agent Harvey turned to Detective Silva and said, "I know what you're worth Silva. But you have to also understand the position this puts SAC Cooper and all the FBI in."

"Oh I get it," Detective Silva said.

"I still need your help so get over to the hospital and get me anything that they have. Pictures, forensics anything. And bring it to this address," Agent Harvey said as he handed Detective Silva a slip of paper with the address to the safe house on it.

Taking the paper from the agent Detective Silva said bristling, "So now I am an errand boy? No, no I understand. Look Agent Harvey, I will do it just let me get over the wound to my pride. I will meet you there later on this afternoon."

"Thank you Silva. You will see that this will all work out in the end."

Turning and walking towards the garage where his car was parked Detective Silva said over his shoulder, "You can count on me Agent Harvey."

At that Detective Silva got in his car and as he turned the key in the ignition of his car, Detective Silva felt his cell phone vibrate. Looking at the caller ID and seeing the unknown caller flash across the screen he gave a sigh before answering, "This is Detective Silva."

A man's voice came across as it had throughout the day, menacing without being directly threatening. "Do you have something for me Detective?"

"What do you want?" The cop replied icily.

When there was no immediate reply from the other end Detective Silva thought that he had gone too far. After all, he had no idea what horrors the man he was talking to was willing to do to him.

"Are you suggesting that I come directly to you and get what I want?" The nameless man said over the phone.

"No," Detective Silva said hurriedly. Then he read the information from the slip of paper that Agent Harvey had given them before he said, "There might only be the two of them and Frank. I don't know how long they plan to..." before he realized that he was talking to a dead line. The man on the other end had already hung up.

A man in a hotel room tossed his phone on the bed next to him and set his watch to wake him later that night. He knew where he would be going and what his task was and had several hours. He turned off the light and slowed his breathing as he prepared to sleep. As he did so he silently hoped that he wouldn't dream, but hoping wasn't to make it so.

The nightmare never changes:

I pull into the driveway of my perfect home. As I get out of my shiny car and look around at the rows of other perfect houses and smile as I walk down to the mailbox. I take a deep breath of the air; fresh cut grass and a sweet smell of the cottonwood tree in the backyard greet me like best friends coming over for dinner. I love the way everything seems so peaceful. I take the mail out of the box and thumb through it as I chuckle to myself. Another notice that Richard Burton has won the Publisher's something or other sweepstakes. How nice would that be to be a multi-millionaire? Mrs. Burton and their daughter would certainly love that. I think to myself as I walk up the never ending driveway that I will have more shoes in my house than any two females can wear in their whole lifetime and somehow the thought makes me sad instead of happy as my sense of humor is something that most people usually notice about me. Finally I make it to the front door and I turn the knob and walk into blackness. It's the middle of the day but inside there is only dark. I call out to my family as I walk through the cold dark house towards the bedroom, "Sweetie! You'll never guess! We are now millionaires and now all the shoe stores will have to pay their employees overtime to keep up with the shopping you and..." And I stop dead in my tracks in the doorway of the bedroom. I see my wife, or what's left of her, naked and in pieces lying on our bedroom floor. Suddenly the metallic smell of blood overwhelms me and I gag. My vision blurs from the tears that fall down my cheeks and with my heart attempting to jump out of my chest and I find myself suddenly running down the hallway towards my daughter's bedroom even though I know what sight is waiting to greet me. The door is open and I peek in, like a little boy trying to catch a glimpse of Santa Clause from the top of the stairway on Christmas morning. I can see the family bible on the floor open to the Book of Revelations and everything is surreal as I see a man bent over my angel. She is staring up with glassy eyes as he grunts while defiling her, and although I can tell she is beyond pain and suffering I can't get my head around the fact that she has gouges in her beautiful face from where some monster has bitten off pieces of her flesh.

Instinct from a former life takes over and I silently step towards the intruder in my home. As I reach out to grab him something in me snaps as a growl escapes my lips –

The man jerks awake in a cold sweat minutes before his alarm was to go off. He gets up and puts on a dark jacket and grabs a black gym bag from under the bed. He walks out of the hotel room door and Hell followed with him.

That evening Agent's Harvey and Hall sat around the kitchen table with their captive, Frank, in an adjoining room of the safe house. It was in a low income part of town, marked by the noise that only poverty can create. With the noise outside it was eerily quiet inside as the two agents pored over the file that Detective Silva had dropped off earlier that day. Not even Frank, who sat on the bed with the tv remote in one hand and the other handcuffed to the bed frame he lay on had much to say.

Agent Hall gave an abrupt start as a dog outside started barking, "I guess I could go for a break, you want anything while I am up?" she said to her partner who looked up from a pile of photos and assorted papers on the table.

"I could take a Pina Colada with an umbrella." Frank said from the bedroom.

"I wasn't talking to you," Agent Hall said. "Besides I am not one of your ho's that waits on you hand and foot in fear of your wrath."

"You don't know what you're missing there sweetie," Frank said as he leered at the female agent.

"That's enough from you Cislo," Agent Harvey said as he got up and walked towards the bedroom.

"Do something for you G-Man?" Frank said sarcastically as Agent Harvey leaned his back against the wall of the bedroom nearest the door.

"Yeah, you can start with telling me the truth."

Laughing, Frank Cislo gave a sneering smile and gave a nod towards the kitchen, "Truth is I would like to get me a piece of that sweet ass you seem to be ignoring."

Sometimes they make it all too easy Agent Harvey thought. "You like that huh?" Making sure that Frank could see, he turned his head to look towards Agent Hall who was bent over at the waist looking in the fridge. He had to admit, she was a remarkably attractive woman and given different circumstances he would be very willing to...*Easy there, just tap into that mentality enough to make him talk to you,* the former BAU Agent thought.

Turning back to look at Frank, Agent Harvey said, "What I don't get about all this is why you? If what you said is true about Vacellaro, then how come he pins all of this on you, and for that reason why on earth would he do that to his own niece, in his own house, on the eve of his own daughter's wedding with all those people there?"

The captive shook his head and snorted with derisive laughter. "You still don't get it G-Man. He has been in prison for years. Have you ever been in lockup?"

"Of course not," Agent Harvey replied.

"Well," Frank continued "When you are in lockup the only thing that keeps you as sane as when you went in is the thing that you want more than anything when you get out. I guess the boss wanted to fuck little girls more than–"

"What the hell?" Agent Hall said right before the unmistakable cough of a suppressed hand gun sounded in the tiny house.

Before Agent Harvey could react he saw his partner thrown back with blood pouring out of a gash in the side of her head. Before any of this registered in his mind he felt his chest explode as a slug ripped into him.

A man in dark clothes was invisible as he made his way from the back yard of a house in a poor section of town.

Crouching under a window he leaned against the cracked wood siding and tried to listen to what was being said inside to better understand what he was up against. He unzipped his bag and pulled out his pistol and silencer, fitting them together like a puzzle. After he checked to be sure he was loaded and ready he stored the bag off to the side to be picked up later when a dog from next door began barking from the porch.

The man slipped around the corner of the house and stepped towards the back door, leveling the point of his gun towards the door. As he waited a moment to ensure that no one was coming to investigate he slipped a lock pick from his pocket and quietly made short work of the ancient lock in the door's handle. He opened the door and slowly slipped into the house like a wraith.

He was a shadow in the darkness, noting two FBI agents in the house standing, one female and one male. They couldn't see him as the lights were out and he was in the living room waiting for the perfect moment.

He saw the female agent turn and open the refrigerator and the male walk into an adjoining room to talk to another man. Listening closely he could make out their conversation perfectly. It always amazed him the things that people said right before they died, and without warning an image flashed in his head of a man on his knees begging for his life, *"Don't kill me please!"*

Blinking his eyes to clear his vision, the man looked again and saw the woman turn from the refrigerator and look at the table covered in photos and files. Without hesitating the man pointed his gun at her head and walked into the light. The woman barely had time to utter a sentence before turning her head at the last minute to look towards her partner. Then he pulled the trigger and saw her head slam backwards and her body crumple onto the floor. He advanced into the kitchen and fired a shot square into the chest of the male FBI agent, noting how surprised he looked before he too fell to the floor.

As the man calmly walked towards the bedroom he looked down at the FBI agent who was sprawled across the doorway.

The man looked into the eyes of the dying man who said between gasps for breath, "Please help me, don't...don't kill me."

Without inflection the man pointed the gun at the agent's head and said, "You don't look so bad. Have another," before coolly pulling the trigger of the silenced weapon ending the dying man's gasping for good.

Deliberately he turned his gaze to the man who was handcuffed to the bed. The man cocked his head to the side as he considered his target with eyes of fire. His target began blubbering with fear saying, "It wasn't fucking me! I swear to God it was that animal Vacellaro, please you got to believe me, it was him! Oh fuck, oh shit!"

"Shh...it will all be over for you soon, Frank," said the man almost lovingly as he pointed the silencer between his target's eyes.

Frank pulled some shred of dignity from his gut as he spat out, "Who the hell are you anyway?"

At that, the last words Frank Cislo ever heard were, "Call me Retribution, Frank." Then Frank saw the flash from the end of the barrel and everything faded to black.

The job he was hired to do now complete and as the only one in the house still left alive the man turned to make his exit. Before he was out of the kitchen though he stopped to look at the collection of papers and photographs on the table that the two FBI agents had been looking at. Noticing the pictures of the little girl, the man gritted his teeth and looked more closely. There he saw something in the scalp that made him pause: An impression of the letter "V" that was quite possibly made from a large diamond ring. The man took the photos and files and made his way out the door. He needed to have a talk with his employer.

Chapter 6
Reprecussions

Detective Silva stood in the kitchen of the safe house noting how different it looked from when he was here last only a few hours ago. Not only because of the federal and local police and medical crew but just the cold feeling that comes with being in a room full of dead bodies. He looked around and noticed that the files he had brought were no where to be found and had an uneasy feeling.

Well, fuck. That's just a perfect end to all this. What the hell did he need with all that?" Detective Silva thought before he heard the low voice from outside calling his name.

When Detective Silva walked outside he noticed the towering SAC walking towards him.

"Is she going to be all right?" Detective Silva asked regarding the injured Agent Hall.

"The doctors don't know yet, but the bullet only grazed her. What do you know about all this?" SAC Cooper asked.

"As little as you do," Detective Silva lied. "I was asked by Agent Harvey to bring some paperwork here from the hospital and after doing so I left."

At that SAC Cooper pointed a finger right in Detective Silva's face, closing the small gap between them with his huge frame and said, "Spare me the bullshit Silva. Do you expect me to believe, for a second that you have nothing to do with this? I have an agent dead, one who may never wake up again and a dead suspect! You and that grease ball family of yours had nothing to do with this? If I ever, in my life, uncover and shred of evidence that points to you I swear to God I am going to throw you and your cousin in prison for the rest of your lives. Do you fucking hear me detective?"

A crowd of police and FBI agents had begun to draw around the two men as SAC Cooper's voice had risen during the conversation. Detective Silva looked around he noticed that he should make him self scarce, or he really will end up in jail. *Not too shocking though, when we were kids 'Zo and I were probably on some of these peoples most wanted list,* Detective Silva thought. Backing away with his hands up he just looked at SAC Cooper before he said, "Hey, you are the one who wanted me out of this investigation. I was willing to help and when your agent asked me to I did what he wanted. Since you don't need me anymore I will leave this to you and your...expertise."

In a rage SAC Cooper rushed the smaller man and would have tackled him if the crowd hadn't stopped him all the while yelling at the detective, "You get the fuck out of my sight you little shit!"

With the big man's shouts fading in the distance, Detective Silva got into his car and made his way down the street back into town. He took out his phone and dialed his cousin Lorenzo.

"Hey 'Zo, its Danny. We need to talk, where are you?" After getting his cousins location, he turned off down a side street and made his way to Lorenzo's house.

Detective Silva pulled into his cousins driveway, and not for the first time appreciated how a life of crime was financially more rewarding than that of a police man. He stepped out of his car and made his way towards the front door, only to be greeted by his cousin who was coming out.

"I hope that you realize the situation that you have put me in 'Zo" Detective Silva said as a greeting.

His cousin took him by the arm and directed him out into the perfectly landscaped front lawn and replied, "I realize that I have never let you down," Lorenzo said to his cousin.

Detective Silva looked his cousin in the eye and asked him, "What are you not telling me that I should know?"

"A very bad thing Danny, are you sure that you want to know? Because once I tell you there is no going back."

With the weight of those words sinking in Detective Silva put his hands on his hips and bowed his head taking deep breaths and said, "What repercussions can I expect to come from all this?"

Lorenzo took his cousin by the shoulders and said softly, "I have not been a saint throughout my life, and I know that you have been by my side through most of it. Trust me when I tell you that what is going to happen tonight will put an end to your part in all of this."

Detective Silva looked up at his cousin and knew that he was right. There had been too many times in their lives that they had put their trust in one another to not do so again. Nodding, Detective Silva asked, "What would you like me to do?"

Lorenzo answered with, "I need you to stay out of Vacellaro's tonight. I have made an arrangement with someone to ensure that that brute never hurts anyone ever again. Other than that…wait for my call."

"Wait for your call?" Detective Silva asked.

"When the task is done I will go to Vacellaro's to confirm. Then I will notify the police, you, since you are the lead detective on the case and my cousin and all you have to do is play according to the rules. Since you wont know what did and what didn't happen, all you will need to do is–"

"Take your statement," Detective Silva finished for his cousin, "I see where you are going with this now. You're right, it's better that I not know."

With nothing left to say the two cousins parted ways. Detective Silva got back into his car and pulled out of the drive and Lorenzo Silva pulled out his phone to make a call. After one ring, a man answered, "Yes?"

Lorenzo made his needs very clear and said, "Tonight Vacellaro will be alone at his estate. I trust that you have the evidence in hand?"

The man on the other end of the phone answered briefly, "Yes," before hanging up. Obviously there was little left for either of them to say.

In his hotel room the man hung up his phone and took out the photos that he had stolen from the safe house. He thumbed through them and tried not to notice how his rage threatened to boil over and consume him. *It never ends,* he thought. He considered the task ahead of him, and from a professional standpoint it didn't seem to pose too many issues. He had the layout of the mansion, and had even been inside. He knew that his mark would be, save for some household staff in a house in the back, alone. *All in all a perfect opportunity* the man thought as he made his preparations to leave the hotel for good.

"And now for the ritual," the lone man in the hotel room said aloud to no one save himself. He changed from his clothes he had worn on his mission the previous night into new ones, storing the old clothes in a trash bag he intended to dump somewhere along the way. He took his bag from under the bed and opening it, pulled out one of half a dozen disposable silencers he had made from fiberglass resin he had picked up at the local hardware store days ago. He fitted it to the Ruger .22 pistol and put them both in a leather case that he had made for that purpose before putting it too into a black gym bag. He took the other handful of silencers and after putting them into yet another trash bag, stepped on them to break them to be disposed of later. He reached into a pocket in the side of the dark gym bag and pulled out a pair of latex gloves and a pair of form fitting black leather gloves, putting the latex ones on first. Then he pulled out a piece of galvanized one inch pipe from the hardware store where he had gotten the fiberglass resin to make the silencers. Noting how it felt comfortable in the grip with the leather gloves he stuffed it too into the gym bag and walked out of the hotel room, making sure to leave the credit card key to the room on the bed as the only reminder that he had ever been there.

Chapter 7
Endgame

At sundown, Paul Vacellaro sat behind his desk comfortable in his huge mansion and felt very satisfied with himself. He had just gotten off the phone with his captain Lorenzo Silva, and had been told that his partner in crime would be arriving later that night to go over some new business, and that the federal nuisance has been dealt with. *It's good to be king,* he thought remembering the line from somewhere but not caring as it suited him to use it for his own purposes. Like so many things Paul Vacellaro was a man who used things that he found interesting and then discarded them when he was done.

As was his habit at night when he was alone, he went to the sound system he had installed in his office and turned on the music. He walked around his office turned off the lights, and stood in front of the bay windows, letting the darkness in the room and the music from the speakers wash over him. He closed his eyes and rolled his massive shoulders to help him relax and began reliving the memory of his last moments with his niece.

She was so young and tender...so, innocent he thought and he felt goose bumps start to prickle on his thick forearms. He took a deep breath and flexed his hands into fists, remembering how it had felt when he had first run his fingers through her long silky hair. He could still smell the scent of her hair, with each deep breath he went deeper into the memory. When suddenly he opened his eyes to find the lights had been turned on.

The man parked his rented car down the street from the Vacellaro estate. He grabbed his bag from the back seat and made his way towards the front gates of the mansion making sure to stay in the shadows even though he was dressed all in black. When he got close to the gates, he pulled a ski mask from the bag he carried and put it on his head to protect his identity from the security cameras around the perimeter. When he got to the gates, he slung the bag over his shoulder and grabbed the bars of the gates. With the skill of a gymnast he hoisted himself over the gates in seconds and then sprinted over the lawn towards the back of the house. When he arrived at the back door, he pulled a key out of his pocket, and fitted it into the lock with a smile and thought, *Sometimes it's all too easy.*

Closing the door behind him, the man dressed all in black made his way from what appeared to be a pantry and into the kitchen. Once there, he knelt down and slung the black bag off his shoulder and opened it. He took the ski mask off, and stored it in the bag before he pulled the leather case from the same bag and carefully extracted his silenced pistol. He then took the pipe out of the bag and zipped it closed before he slung it back onto his shoulder. Making sure that the bag was firmly in place he picked up the tools of his trade, the pipe in his right hand and the pistol in his left. As the man walked across the kitchen he was about to pass into the dining room when something caught his eye. He noticed what looked like a magnetic knife holder attached to the wall and on it a huge cleaver. As he got closer he could see, even in the dark, that it held a viciously sharp edge. Slowly a grin came to the man's face as a plan began to form in his mind.

Inspiration for a perfect end, the man thought to himself. He put down the silenced pistol and took the cleaver from the magnet that held it to the wall. He then carefully stored the cleaver in one of the cargo pockets of his black military style pants before he picked up the pistol and made his way into the dining room. Once he was in there, he passed by the extravagant dining table, and into the foyer at the front of the house. He gave a cursory glance towards the front door to make sure that he wouldn't be spotted going up the stairs he made his way to the top. As he got closer to the top of the stairway, he could hear music drifting from what would be Vacellaro's office. He cautiously crept towards the office door and waited.

The man strained his ears but could only hear the music, so he stepped in front of the door, and noticed it was open a crack and there was no light coming from inside. He opened the door so he could just see inside and there he noticed Paul Vacellaro himself standing in front of a window with his back to him. Moving as silent as a shadow despite the sound of the music coming from the speakers the man went through the open door and pushed it closed with his heel making sure not to lose sight of the massive target in front of him.

And now the beginning of the end, the man thought to himself as he raised the pistol and pointed the silenced weapon at Vacellaro's back before flipping the switch to turn on the lights. Before Vacellaro could turn around the man squeezed the trigger and sent a round into his target's kidney knowing the pain of being shot in the kidney is such that he would be unable to scream. Before

Vacellaro hit the ground the man had dropped his pistol to the floor and began advancing on the huge man as he struggled to his knees.

Vacellaro didn't have a chance to even see his attacker before he felt another flash of pain as the man swung the pipe with all his strength and struck the writhing mobster in the same bloody spot the bullet had pierced.

"Now that I have your attention, there is something that I want to talk to you about," the man with the pipe said over the sound of the music.

With all his strength Paul Vacellaro turned and saw the man who was standing over him and at recognizing him as the hit man he had met just days ago his face drained of color.

"What the fuck are you doing in my house?" Vacellaro asked with a tremble in his voice.

With a smile the man thought *I love it when they ask me that.*

"Allow me to show you something, Paul," the man said almost conversationally before he swung the pipe again and this time struck Vacellaro across the shoulders. As Vacellaro grunted in pain and rolled around on the ground unable to move, the man took the bag off his shoulder and placed it on the desk beside him. He opened the bag while keeping an eye on his target and reached in to pull out a manila folder. He held the folder over Vacellaro and allowed the photos to drop down one after the other onto the floor next to the mobster who was slowly bleeding into the carpet.

"Notice anything familiar rapist?" The man asked as he towered over the bleeding grunting once all powerful mobster.

When Vacellaro wasn't forthcoming with an answer, the man took a deep breath and let out an audible sigh before he said with his flat affect, "Perhaps you didn't hear me. Allow me to ask you again," then the man swung the pipe with a flick of his wrist and heard an audible *Crack!* as the metal of the pipe struck Vacellaro in the side of his head.

At this point Paul Vacellaro knew that it was fight back, or die and acted accordingly. Through a blur of vision he tried to struggle to his hands and knees but the carpet was drenched with his blood and his hands slipped in the blood soaked carpet.

The man saw that Paul Vacellaro still had some fight left in him and thought, *No, it ends here.* With a *whoosh,* the man brought the pipe down again and again on Vacellaro's head asking the same question as before and striking the writhing child rapist on the floor.

"Do." *Crack!* "You." *Crack!* "Notice." *Crack!* "Anything" *Crack!* "Familiar?" *Crack!* As the man stood over the bloody mess that once was Small Paul Vacellaro breathing hard with the exertion of swinging the pipe he took notice that the tough fear inspiring mobster was no longer moving, not even to breathe.

His job almost done, the man tossed the bloody pipe to the floor and pulled out the cleaver from his cargo pocket. The man dressed in black then knelt down and took hold of Vacellaro's hand and promptly cut off the finger with the diamond encrusted "V" on it. Sawing through the bone was no different than cutting through warm butter and when he was done the man carefully took the disjointed finger and lightly placed it next to the photos that littered the floor.

If the police can't figure out that clue then they do not deserve to call themselves police, the man thought to him self disdainfully as he stood and dusted off his hands superficially, as though to rid him self of the blood that had sprayed onto him from his earlier work. Right then the music ended and the man allowed himself a smile and thought, *how appropriate,* before he turned to leave the room. That's when he saw Lorenzo Silva standing in the doorway, with the man's silenced pistol right at his feet.

For a brief moment the two men stood facing each other, neither of them taking their eyes off of the other. Without any trace of fear the man nodded his head towards the well dressed Silva and walked towards him picking up the pipe and silenced weapon.

The man didn't say a word as he made to brush past his employer, but Silva cleared his throat and said in a voice barely more than a whisper "There will be significant fallout from such a mess like this. I could use a man such as you to keep the...peace, while the transition takes place."

Turning his head deliberately and looking directly into Silva's eyes the man said, "Our business is over, you've had your retribution" before shouldering past and walking calmly down the hallway towards the top of the grand stairway.

Lorenzo Silva watched the man disappear into the darkness of the mansion and when he was sure that the man had left and he was alone he pulled out his phone to call his cousin Detective Silva to tell him that the nightmare was over and the demon was dead.

Epilogue

For the second time in less than a week, Lorenzo Silva stood at the top of the stairs in Vacellaro's mansion as a crowd of federal agents, police, medical crew and reporters gathered in all corners of the spacious house.

"It's hard to believe that this was almost the exact same scene only a few days ago," Detective Silva said, echoing his cousins thoughts.

Turning his head to look at the cop who was as close as a brother Lorenzo said, "But this time there will be a happier ending. To be sure it will be difficult to maintain control of the crew without their fear of Vacellaro, but I think that I will manage to make the best of it."

Detective Silva shook his head and said, "Are you really trying to tell me this? You know better, I ought to arrest you on the spot."

Lorenzo smiled at his cousin and the two men shared a quiet laugh as he remembered how so many times they had had that same conversation.

Sobering quickly, Detective Silva said, "Seriously though you should watch yourself. I know that you are capable enough but I don't want to have to visit you in jail.

Just think of how that will go over when I have to sit across from your family at holidays knowing where you are."

"Don't worry about that, I have everything under control," Lorenzo replied.

Detective Silva started walking down the stairs towards the front door of the house when he stopped and turned to look up to his cousin and said, "You are still coming over this weekend right?"

"I wouldn't miss it for the world," Lorenzo said.

In another city a man pulled his rented car into a convenience store parking lot, and stepped out. He was dressed in brown pants and a long sleeve button down shirt and looked like anyone else in any other city in the country. He walked towards the door and before he could pull it open he had to dodge out of the way of another man bursting out of the door.

The non-descript man stepped to the side and heard the man who had just come from inside mutter something, "Fucking bitch," before he got into his car and drove away screeching his tires as he went out into the street.

The ordinary man shook his head and walked through the door into the cool interior of the little store. When the glass door shut behind him and closed out the noise from the city, he could hear someone crying. He walked towards the counter and noticed a petite woman standing with her head bowed and her shoulders shaking as she silently sobbed into her shirt.

The man cleared his throat to announce that he was there, and immediately the woman looked up embarrassed.

"I'm sorry," she said dabbing at her eyes with the sleeve of her shirt, "how can I help you sir?"

The man looked at her name tag that was slightly askew and saw her name before he looked up and said with surprising gentleness considering who he was and what he did, "Cindy. My mothers name was Cindy. Are you all right?"

With a rush of embarrassment Cindy said, "I am just being silly. I will be fine." But the man knew that she wouldn't. Without saying anything he just raised an eyebrow and let the silence between them break her will.

"The guy who you must have just missed was an ex-boyfriend. I have been trying to hide from him for a while and now that he has found me he said that he was going to follow me home and beat on me and kill me. I just can't take the abuse anymore and I swear he would have if I hadn't been here where people could just walk in," The woman named Cindy said as she broke down in tears all over again.

She continued "I can't even call the police because he has so many friends there and they all cover for him. God, I wish he would just leave me alone. Dammit, why am I even saying this to you?" she said before the sobs got too bad that she couldn't talk.

The man looked at the crying woman and put his hands on the counter and leaned forward. He looked deliberately at the woman and said to her in a very serious voice, "Cindy? Look at me. I am going to ask you a question and I want you to think very hard before you answer, okay?"

"Okay," Cindy replied.

Nodding his head once the man asked Cindy in a flat voice that would later chill her to the bone with the memory of what it meant, "Would you like to have retribution?"

THE END

CPSIA information can be obtained at www.ICGtesting.com
Printed in the USA
BVOW01s1236230816

459895BV00001B/23/P